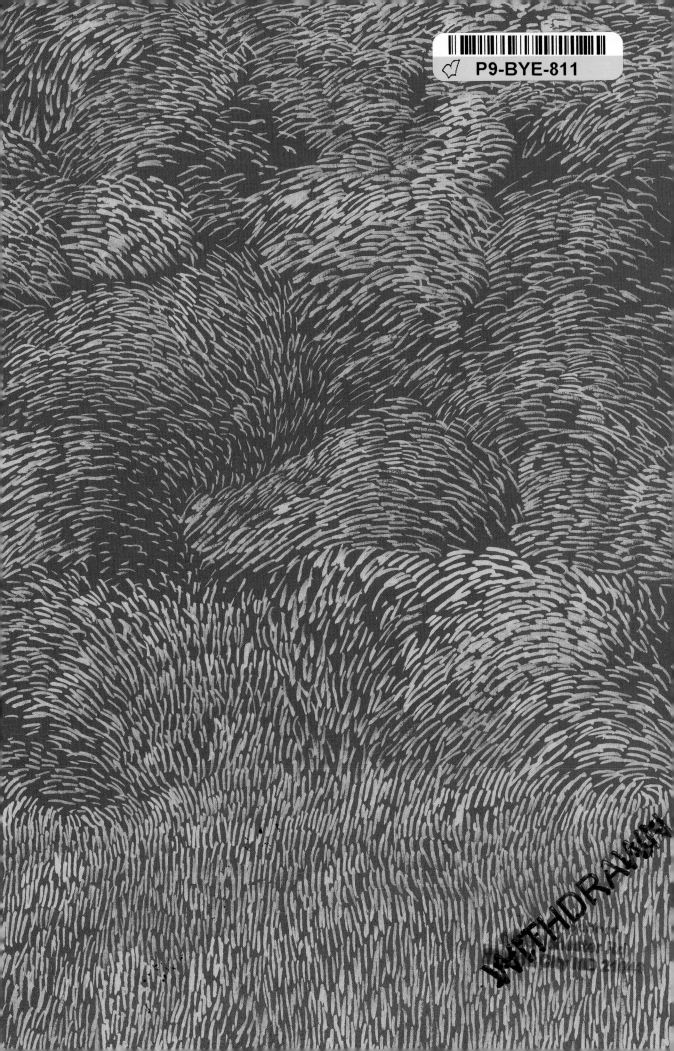

AUTHOR'S NOTE

Won Ton's story is told in a series of senryu (SEN-ree-yoo), a form of Japanese poetry developed from and similar to haiku (HI-koo). Both senryu and haiku typically feature three unrhymed lines containing a maximum of seventeen syllables (5-7-5, respectively); each form also captures the essence of a moment. In haiku, that moment focuses on nature. In senryu, however, the foibles of human nature—or in this case, cat nature—are the focus, expressed by a narrator in a humorous, playful, or ironic way.

In memory of Beaujolais and Riesling
And to our new shelter kitties: Mai Tai, Papaya, and Koloa
—L. W.

To Laura, Sally, and Patrick
—E. Y.

Henry Holt and Company, LLC
Publishers since 1866
175 Fifth Avenue
New York, New York 10010
mackids.com

Library of Congress Cataloging-in-Publication Data
Wardlaw, Lee.
Won-Ton : a cat tale told in haiku / by Lee Wardlaw ; illustrated by Eugene Yelchin. — 1st ed.
p.   cm.
Summary: A cat arrives at a shelter, arranges to go home with a good family, and settles in with them,
all the while letting them know who is boss and, finally, sharing his real name.
ISBN 978-0-8050-8995-0
[1. Cat adoption—Fiction. 2. Cats—Fiction. 3. Haiku.] I. Yelchin, Eugene, ill. II. Title.
PZ7.W2174Won 2010   [E]—dc22   2009029414

First Edition—2011 / Designed by Elizabeth Tardiff
The artist used graphite and gouache on watercolor paper to create the illustrations for this book.
Printed in China by Macmillan Production (Asia) Ltd., Kwun Tong, Kowloon, Hong Kong (supplier code 10)

5 7 9 10 8 6 4

WON TON

A Cat Tale Told in Haiku

Lee Wardlaw

illustrated by

Eugene Yelchin

Henry Holt and Company
New York

The Shelter

Nice place they got here.

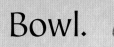 Bed.

Bowl.

Blankie.

Just like home!

Or so I've been told.

Gypsy on my left.
Pumpkin, my right. Together,
we are all alone.

Visiting hours!
Yawn. I pretend not to care.

Yet—I sneak a peek.

The Choosing

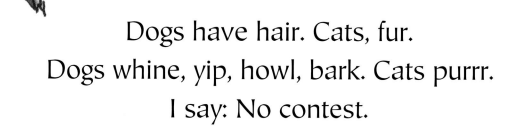

Dogs have hair. Cats, fur.
Dogs whine, yip, howl, bark. Cats purrr.
I say: No contest.

I dub her Pinchy.
He's—OW!—Tail-Yanker. You, Boy,
rub my chin just right.

No rush. I've got plans.
Gnaw this paw. Nip that flea. And
wish: Please, Boy, pick me.

Latch squeaks. Door swings wide.
Free! Free at last! Yet, one claw
snags, clings to what's known.

The Car Ride

Letmeoutletme
outletmeoutletmeout.
Wait—let me back in!

The Naming

Buster? Bubba? SPIKE?
Great Rats! Those don't befit an
Oriental prince.

Cleo. Leia. Belle.
Got a tick in your ear? I
said prince, not princess.

Won Ton? How can I
be soup? Some day, I'll tell you
my real name. Maybe.

The New Place

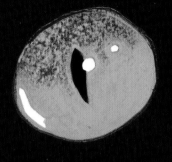

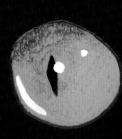

Deep, dark bed cave. Me?
Hiding? I'm no scaredy-cat!
I like dust bunnies!

"Here, kitty, kitty."
Ha. I'll stay put till I know:
Are they friend . . . or foe?

Yawn. String-on-a-stick.
Fine. I'll come out and chase it
to make you happy.

The Feeding

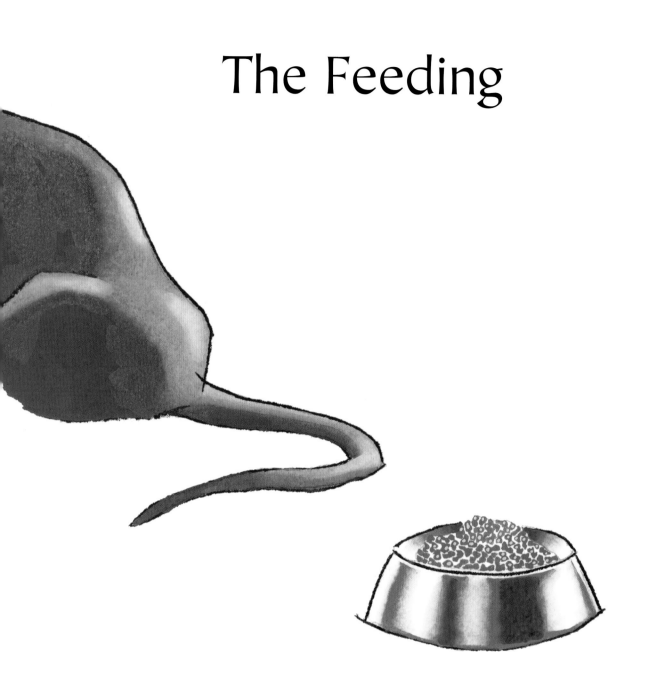

Sniff. Snub. What is this
stuff? True, I liked it once. That
was then, this is now.

Fine. If you insist.
I'll try Just.One.Nibble. But—
I won't enjoy it.

What do you mean "Ewww"?
How is my tuna breath worse
than peanut butter?

Sorry about the
squishy in your shoe. Must've
been something I ate.

The Adjustment

Scrat-ching-post? Haven't
heard of it. Besides, the couch
is so much closer.

Pesky fly! Allow
me to muzzle his buzzle.
Never mind the lamp.

Naptime! Begone, oh fancy pad. I prefer these socks. They smell of you.

Help! I've been catnapped,
dressed in frillies, forced to lap
tea with your sister.

Letmeoutletme
outletmeoutletmeout.
Wait—let me back in!

The Yard

A dog stopped here once.
And here. There. And here again.
Oh, a cat's nose knows!

Crickets crunch. Mice snap.
Wing thing makes a dusty snack:
No meat on a moth.

Prickle-puffed, I hiss:
Ssscat! This yard ain't big enough
for the both of us.

Letmeinletme
inletmeinletmein.
Wait—let me back out!

Home

Hel-looo. I'm waiting.
Put down that pesky pencil
and fetch the catnip.

I explained it loud
and clear. What part of "meow"
don't you understand?

Oops! I mistook these
for wiggly worms. I didn't
know they were your toes.

Eavesdropping, I hear:
"My cat." Great Rats! Don't you know
yet that you're My Boy?

Your tummy, soft as
warm dough. I knead and knead, then
bake it with a nap.

"Good night, Won Ton," you
whisper. Boy, it's time you knew:
My name is Haiku.

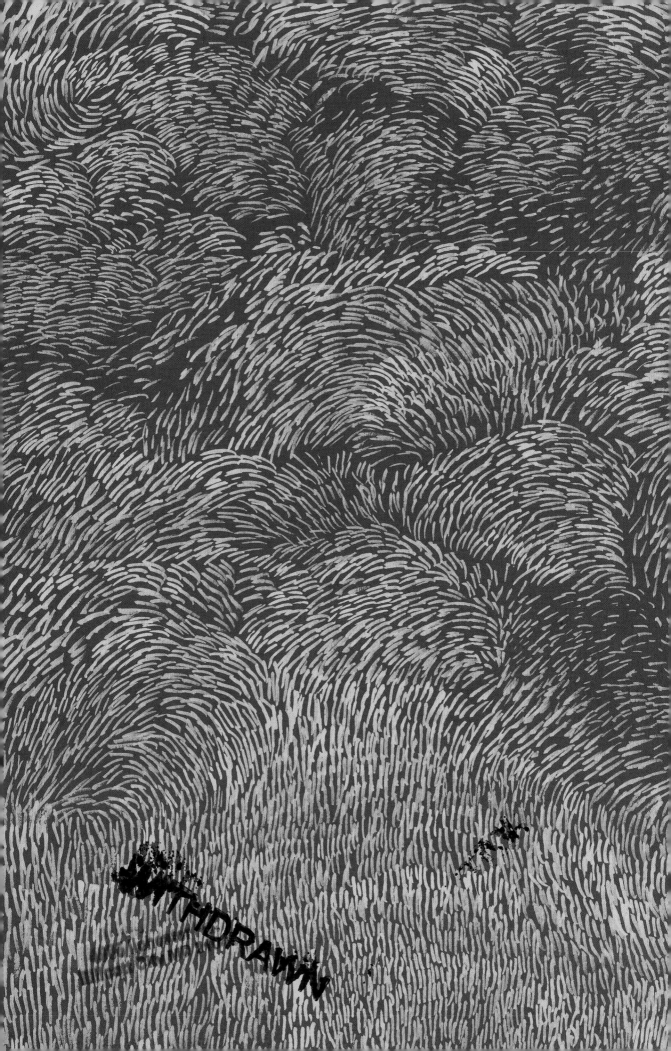